Pete the Popcorn

Sarviol Publishing

ISBN: 978-1468036466

Special wholesale and re-sale rates are available.
For more information, please contact
Deb Harvest at
petethepopcorn@gmail.com

When purchasing this book, please consider purchasing
an additional copy to donate to your local library.

THE Pete Popcorn

Written by Nick Rokicki & Joseph Kelley
Illustrated by Kathleen Smith Waters

Dec 2013

William

ALWAYS Right

ALWAYS Encourage

Pete was a Popcorn kernel.

I know it sounds silly, but
Popcorns have playful lives, too.

It was early October and Pete had been punching in at Popcorn Prep for a whole month!

1+1=2
2+2=4
3+3=6
4+4=8
5+5=10

Every day was filled with Popcorn Math,...

...and Pete's least-favorite subject, Popcorn Pre-History.

On this day, Pete the Popcorn just didn't feel like getting out of his pod.

Something was on his mind and he just didn't feel too peppy, like Popcorns normally should.

Pete's neighbor, Patty the pale Popcorn, knocked on the door to Pete's pad.

"Come on, Pete! It's a perfect day! Today we're going to learn the secrets to performing the perfect pop," Patty said.

"I just don't feel too perky today, Patty... You go on without me," replied Pete.

Patty didn't like the pitch in Pete's voice.

15

"What's the problem, Pete ?" asked
Patty, as she pushed open the door.

"Don't be a punk! We have to
persist in our positive point-of-view!"

Pete says, "It's just that all of us Popcorns are the same!

We're all the same size, shape, and color! And we all want to be popped and eaten someday... so how do we stand out enough to be chosen? What is going to make me different enough to be popped and turned into something really delicious?"

"Well, Pete-- we may all seem the same physically, but it's our attitude and sense of purpose that make us really special! We'll all get eaten, Pete-- because that's what we're here for," Patty went on, "sure, everybody in our class grew up on the same ear, but you're a special little kernel because I think you're the smartest one around..."

"You do? Promise?"

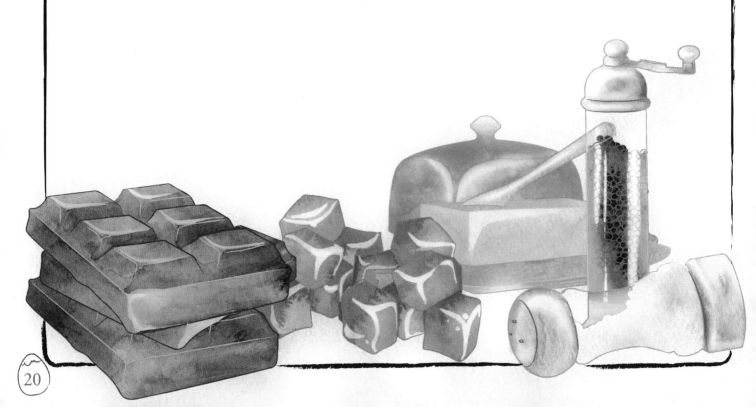

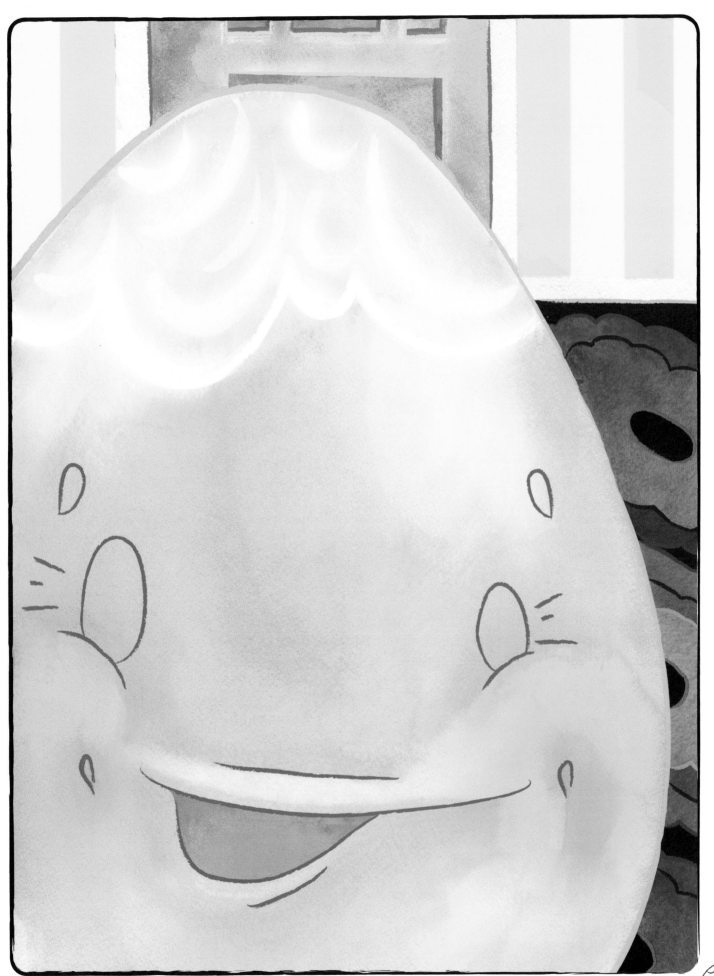

Pete's little heart pitter-pattered and the next thing he knew, he was perched in class at Popcorn Prep, with Patty by his side.

Professor Popcorn was presenting photos of different and scrumptious-looking Popped Popcorn!

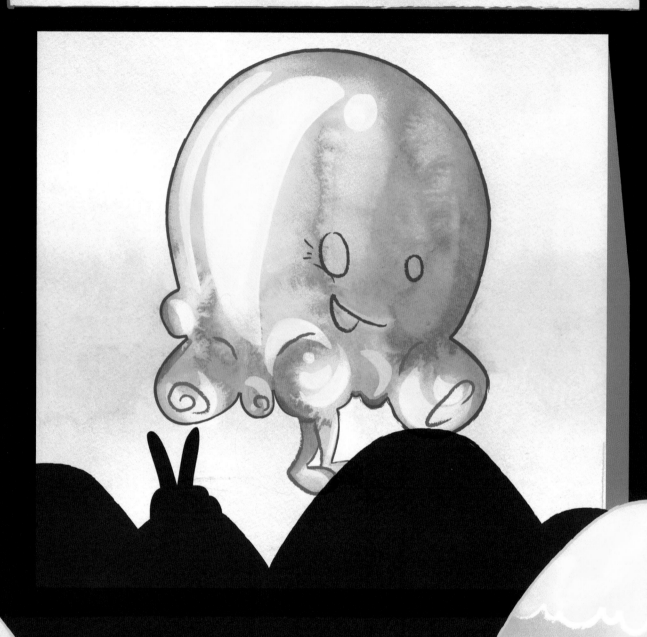

"You can pop up to be a caramel corn."

"Or you might pop up to be a pecan praline popcorn."

Some little kernels even pop up and become popcorn that are presented with little pieces of bacon," said Professor Popcorn!

Pete's eyes grew **wide** as the pictures passed by.

He turned to Patty and proclaimed, **"you're right!**

We might all be the same now...
But we can pop up into
anything we want to be!

I want to pop up and be a
chocolate-covered popcorn!

Or a **particular** popcorn
with only *Pacific* sea salt!

Or a popcorn packaged with **peanuts** or **pretzels**! Or a...."

KITCHEN

Pete continued to name all of the
possibilities for his popped future.
And Patty looked pleased.

And this is the plain and simple plan that prepared Pete for a most paramount lesson of growing up-- we all pop into a perfect future for our personality!

A Note from Joe Kelley...

When thinking about dedications for this book, I was reminded of stories from the past. I have crossed paths with and met some wonderful people in my life, both family and friends. So here go the stories!

Nanny, the best grandmother ever: I remember us walking from your house on Hunter to Westland Mall, where we would get Sander's Ice Cream. Hot Fudge Cream Puffs for both of us (no chocolate for me) and then it was off to Quo Vadis to see a movie. Almost every positive memory from my childhood involves you. Thank you for teaching me to be considerate of others and always being there to give me a hug. I think about you every single day and cannot wait to see you again. Nanny, I love you and thank you for everything.

Mom: Thank you for teaching me that being different is a good thing. I appreciate all the sacrifices you made as a young mother to raise me. I will always remember you reading to me every night, no matter how exhausted you were. You'll be in my heart forever and I'm so glad you're here to teach your grandchildren all of the same lessons that you taught me. I love you more than anything!

Sarah: My younger sister, I remember rocking you as a baby and how you would wake up every hour. How did I survive with this new screaming baby? Thanks for all your support over the years. I love you and hope happiness is always with you--- you deserve it!

David: My little brother. Once a US Marine, always a US Marine. Taken from us all at age 20, I feel your life was cut short. God, however, often has a different plan. I remember the last night I was able to hang out with you, at a pub near the University of Michigan. It remains one of my favorite days. Thanks for the smiles that you still bring to me... and remember that when I see you again, I have a crazy haircut in store for you-- like you did once to me! We all miss you so much.

Deanna: My youngest sister, when you were 5 or 6 years old, you were wearing roller skates and you came flying into Nanny's house, directly in front of the steps leading down. When you almost fell down the steps, I scolded you and told you to be careful. Your reply? "I don't have to listen to you! You're not my teacher!" And from that day on... you've never once listened to me. Shoot for the stars and never take "no" for an answer! Love you.

Hayden: My first and only nephew, from the moment I held you, I was truly happy. You are the most curious and talkative boy I've ever seen. Your curiosity and never-ending search for answers will take you very far. In my wallet, I still carry the photo of you at age 5 with Riley, who was just about

10 weeks old. I love you, Hayden!

Aleksondra: In memory of my first niece, whose time with us was short. In my mind, I still hear the way you would say, "Joe-Joe!" There would be exaggerated G's and an occasional Z sound. Go to the library in Heaven and pick up this book, my little angel.

Davie: My little niece, such a shy and sweet girl--- until you get to know her… then she is playful and funny as can be! Thank you for always being ready with a big hug as you also yell, "Joe-Joe," so much like your sister. It makes me grin from ear to ear every time you ask about Riley. Be forever innocent and always do what makes you happy!

Auntie Shirl: Thanks for always making me laugh. Those days when you would take me out of school and proceed to Taco Bell for lunch were my favorite! You made so many childhood memories fun for me--- and nobody can make fun of my Mom like you can!

Sissy: My aunt, your handicap wasn't a burden to me at all. In fact, learning the struggles and the challenges you faced in your life taught me compassion. I remember your laugh when you would hold a baby or your smile when we would read you a book. I can picture you in Heaven, running and jumping through the clouds.

Auntie Deb: My Aunt by choice, you have influenced me by always being yourself! You've always shown me that standing up for yourself is the most important tool. You never let that 5'3" frame (in heels) stand in your way! Thanks for teaching me courage and respect.

Cheryl Betz: The perfect example of a true friend. Thanks for all the adventures we've been on. Your father would be so proud of the woman you've become and the family you have grown. All I have to say is, "Easter Pig!" Love ya!

Jennifer Buczek: Best of friends for over a decade… who could forget the late night chats over Denny's? Nobody can make fun of themselves like you can. I wish you and your family only the best.

Jerry Jones: Your wit and sarcasm has always been your charm. Thanks for always standing by me, no matter the circumstances. Your parents did a fine job.

Karen Billings: In loving memory of my neighbor. Your smile and beauty will never leave you. Thank you for years of laughter and good times.

Paula Gnacke (Gnacker): What haven't we been through? Thank you for teaching me to be unselfish-- and to treat others how we would want to be treated. Thanks for the countless memories that rush into my head whenever your name is mentioned.

Daniel Green: A childhood friend who taught me the greatest lesson of not caring what others may think. You are remembered for your kindness and gentle ways.

Cheryl Magewick: I'll never eat cookies in Key West again… or cry on a golf cart. Red Fish and I know who to call when we need a laugh.

Debbie Garrity: I knew we would be friends for life from our first moments together at the Schoolcraft Craft Show. And you make awesome websites for your best friends!

Shelly Erikson: Memories of driving around in your convertible abound. I hope we can continue to have fun!

Kathleen Smith Waters: Our illustrator who came to us through a total fluke conversation with her awesome cousin, Becky Smith... you brought Pete to life and I cannot thank you enough.

Riley: To the cutest dog in the world... you've made life more fun.

Special mentions to the children and extended families in my life: London DeRue, Madison and Hayden Martin, Gemma Jett and Keatyn Reine Veilleux, Riley and Nick Porter, Emma and Grace Shirley, Hailie Kittner, Cameron and Alyssa Downes, Brayden and Brynlee Pratt, Dan Dipple, The Smith Family, The Kittner Family, The Fox Family, Ivan Harris, Jeff Mineau, JJ Megge, Rick and Jessica, Duck, Milton, Ivy, Maria, Cecile and Dennis Webber, The Olrich Family, The Lohr Family, Judy Governo, Kathy Johnson, Casey Coon, John Glenn Class of 1990, friends from the movie theater, my Maui family (including Kia, Estella, Lex and Danny Brown), the teachers and students of Edison Elementary and John Marshall Junior High, along with everyone at Schoolcraft College and Madonna University and TEAM PETE Members.

To learn more about Joe Kelley, please visit ABOUT THE AUTHORS at www.PeteThePopcorn.com

A Note from Nick Rokicki...

I've always loved to write. In fact, when my 7th grade history teacher, Mr. Heindorff, signed my yearbook, he wrote, "Nick-- will you be a politician or a writer?" I'd like to think there might be time for both.

There is no chance this book would have come about without the influence of the original writer in the family-- my grandmother, Violet Olrich. She was the editor of her school newspaper. And I really do believe that from her is where I got my creative writing bug. I think about her and my Grandpa Myrel on a daily basis.

Also, I'm hoping that while promoting this book, I can take a lesson from my father, Leon Rokicki. He could talk to anyone-- about anything. And that's what I hope I can do all across the country at festivals and fairs, as I meet you and your kids-- let's carry on a conversation. I want to learn something from this whole process... and hopefully you can be the one to teach it to me.

My mother, Sandy Rokicki, is the one that always taught me the primary message in Pete the Popcorn: you can do anything you want with your life. You can grow up and be whatever you want and follow what dreams may come. Without my Mom telling me this in subtle ways over the years, I wouldn't have tried half the things I have in my short time on Earth so far. Thanks, Mom.

Our good friend Debbie Garrity also deserves a heartfelt mention. Without her encouragement, constant creativity and silly laughter--- I may have stopped being artistic a long time ago. Thanks, Debbie.

All of the flight attendants, pilots and the local DTW management at Pinnacle Airlines must also be mentioned, along with the thousands of passengers that I've met. I've had an awesome 8 years flying around this country, meeting character after character. Plus those flight benefits come in handy. Sharon Schultz, Rick and Jessica, Susan Dougherty, Kathleen DiCicco, Debra Fair, Chad Whitaker and so many more--- you make work fun.

Finally-- Joe. If you wouldn't have said those fateful words, "let's write a Children's Book," Pete would have never popped onto the page. Let's make this the last crazy business venture, though. Ok?

This page would not be complete without a special thanks to the world's greatest candy-cane-thief and illustrator, Kathleen Smith Waters. I wish you could have seen the smile on my face every time a new page would arrive.

Pete the Popcorn is dedicated to all of the young readers out there… especially those in Toledo, Ohio. The most important young readers in my life are my nieces, Terra Marquis and MacKenzie Moran. And my nephews, Thomas Marquis and Travis Miles. Don't forget-- never quit learning and dream big. Every opportunity and hope for the future awaits you.

To learn more about Nick Rokicki, please visit ABOUT THE AUTHORS at www.PeteThePopcorn.com

A Note from Kathleen Smith Waters...

I would like to thank my parents for always standing by me and supporting me. My cousin Becky Smith, none of this would be possible without you! I would like to thank my professors at the Cleveland Institute of Art, Dominic Scibilia and John Chuldenko for helping me become the artist that I am today. Lastly, I would like to thank Pete!